W9-BJP-616

The CRYSTAL MOUNTAIN

Retold and Illustrated by RUTH SANDERSON

Little, Brown and Company
Boston   New York   London

ong ago in a land far away, there lived a woman named Anna who wove brocaded cloth to support her three sons and herself. Some people said the birds and flowers in her designs were more beautiful than real ones. Merchants were eager to buy her brocades, for there was a great demand among the noble classes for garments made from such finely woven fabrics.

Leon, Anna's eldest son, loaded the heavy rolls of fabric onto the cart to sell in a nearby city. He was known as one of the strongest young men in the kingdom. Blaine, her second son, was known for his great intelligence and always made a fine profit selling his mother's goods. The two made fun of their youngest brother, Perrin, whose favorite activity was making up songs on his lute.

"He plans to play for the king!" Leon mocked him one morning as they climbed onto the cart.

"We'll return in a week or so, as usual, Mother," said Blaine, as he pulled Perrin up beside him on the seat.

"Fare thee well," she called as they drove off to the city.

That night, Anna dreamed of a place more beautiful than any she had ever seen. A white marble mansion stood surrounded by exquisite gardens. Birds flew among ancient oak trees and sang in orchards and grape arbors. A stream wound through rolling hills. There was even a pond with a pair of swans floating among yellow lilies. It looked like a paradise.

When Anna woke, the dream was still clear, and she longed with all her heart to live there. *I must see that place before I die,* she thought. *If I cannot go there, then I will weave a picture of it in cloth.*

When her sons returned home, they found Anna working at her loom. At night the light of a crude oil lamp burned her eyes, and as her tears fell onto the threads, she wove them into the streams and the lily pond. As days turned into months, her sons expressed their concern.

"I will have to cut firewood to earn a living," complained Leon, who was strong but lazy.

"Our funds are getting much too low!" worried Blaine, for he loved the sound of coins in the coffer.

Perrin composed songs and sang for his mother while she worked. He alone understood her need. One year became two, and still she wove, hardly eating or sleeping. At the end of the third year, the tapestry was finally done. Leon hung it on the wall, and they all gathered around to admire it. Anna smiled, for it was exactly like her dream.

As Anna gazed happily at her creation, a breeze came through the window and raised a corner of the tapestry. Then a strong gust lifted it off the wall and blew it out the open door. Anna and her sons ran after it and watched in amazement as the wind carried it away. It flew far to the east, then disappeared from sight.

"You must find my tapestry," Anna entreated her sons, "for it is my life!"

Leon set out at once. After three days, he came upon a hermit sitting outside a cave.

"What is it that you seek?" asked the old man.

Leon told him what had happened to his mother's tapestry.

"The wind obeys the Fairies of the Crystal Mountain," the hermit said. "They admired your mother's tapestry and have taken it so that they can make a copy."

"Tell me the way to the Crystal Mountain," demanded Leon.

"The way is hard," said the hermit. "First you must cross a fiery plain. If you so much as utter a cry, the flames will engulf you. Then you must cross an icy sea. Again, you will perish if you make a sound. Lastly you must climb the treacherous Crystal Mountain to reach the fairies' palace."

Leon turned pale at the thought of facing such obstacles.

"If the way is too difficult for you, here is a bag of gold that you might find useful," said the hermit. Strong of body but weak-willed, Leon took the gold. Ashamed to return home without the tapestry, he went instead to the city.

When a month passed and Leon did not return home, Blaine set out to find the tapestry. He, too, came upon the hermit and learned where he needed to go to find it. Blaine called the hermit a silly old fool, for his superior logic told him that no ordinary man could survive a fiery plain and an icy sea, let alone scale a mountain of crystal. He readily accepted the bag of gold offered by the hermit. Embarrassed by his failure, Blaine sought the city as well.

A month later, Perrin left his mother in the care of their kind neighbors, for she was sick with worry.

"Be careful, my son," Anna said as she watched her youngest begin the quest for her precious weaving. Perrin traveled to the east and reached the hermit's cave. He listened as the hermit described the trials of fire and ice and the great Crystal Mountain.

"I will set out at once," Perrin said, "and somehow I will retrieve my mother's tapestry."

"Wait," said the hermit. "I have something for you."

He handed Perrin not a bag of gold but a silver whistle on a string.

"Blow this when you have a need," the hermit said.

Perrin set off to the east and soon came to the fiery plain. He blew once on the
hermit's whistle, and a magnificent black horse in black armor appeared. A suit
of matching armor hung from the saddle. Perrin put it on and mounted the
black steed.

They plunged into the fire, and though it was hot, the armor made it bearable and Perrin did not cry out. When they finally broke free of the flames, Perrin collapsed upon the ground. Immediately the brave young man fell asleep, and when he woke, the horse and armor were gone.

In a few days, Perrin reached the icy sea, which stretched out endlessly before him. Again he blew the whistle. With a snort and a neigh, a huge white charger galloped up behind him. Its silver armor gleamed in the sun. Perrin put on the matching armor that was hanging on the saddle.

As soon as he mounted, the horse leaped into the icy sea. The waves crashed against them, and Perrin clung to the horse's neck. The cold was almost unbearable, but with the help of the armor, he was able to endure it. After what seemed like hours, horse and rider reached the far shore. Perrin tumbled to the sand and fell into a deep sleep.

He woke as the sun rose and saw that the second horse had disappeared like the first. Gleaming in the distance was the Crystal Mountain, which seemed to be there and not there at the same time. Through it Perrin could see other mountains and clouds and sky. The palace at the summit seemed to float in the clouds. In a matter of hours Perrin had reached its base. He could not imagine how to climb the sheer sides, so he blew the whistle for the third time.

A third horse appeared, more magnificent than the others. It was a blood red bay wearing a golden saddle and bridle. A red cloak hung from its saddle. The great horse reared when Perrin mounted, and its iron-studded hooves left a spray of crystal fragments as it leaped up the mountain. When they reached the top, Perrin dismounted and stole into the fairies' palace.

Perrin heard singing and laughter and followed the sound to a great hall. There his mother's tapestry hung next to an enormous loom. All around the room were fairies, singing, playing lutes and other instruments, chatting and laughing

in musical tones. When they saw Perrin, they fell silent and stared at him.

"I have come for my mother's tapestry," Perrin declared.

The fairy weaving at the loom turned to look at him.

The fairy was dressed in red and gold and had a friendlier appearance than the others. Perrin liked her at once.

A tall, haughty fairy approached Perrin and said, "We will finish weaving our copy tonight, and *perhaps* tomorrow you may take your mother's tapestry home."

As it grew dark, the fairies wandered off one by one until Perrin was alone with the Red Fairy. He picked up a lute left behind by one of the fairies and began to play. The Red Fairy smiled as she continued to weave, and sang along with him in a sweet, haunting voice. When he could play no more, Perrin dropped off to sleep.

The Red Fairy finished the brocade and stood up to look at her work. The original was more lifelike and had more spirit. She looked from Anna's tapestry to Perrin sleeping nearby. It made her sad to think that soon they would be gone. Taking up a needle and thread, she embroidered a picture of herself next to the lily pool on Anna's tapestry. Then she rolled it up and placed it near the sleeping lute player.

Perrin woke before dawn with his mother's tapestry neatly rolled up beside him. He grabbed it and ran outside before the other fairies could wake and give chase. Once again, Perrin blew the silver whistle and the bay horse appeared. The wind swirled around them and lifted horse and rider into the air, tapestry and all. Perrin held on with all his might as they flew over the icy sea and the fiery plain, arriving home in just a few hours' time.

Anna rose from the front steps to greet her son with joy. Perrin unrolled the tapestry that was so precious to his mother. Then an amazing thing happened.

The threads of the tapestry seemed to tremble, and the picture began to expand, soon covering all the land in sight. The shining stream flowed among hills where real sheep and cattle grazed, birds darted in and out of trees laden with fruit. Where the cottage had just stood, there was now a white marble mansion. Next to the lily pool sat a beautiful girl in a red dress.

It was the fairy who had woven herself into the brocade. By doing so, her magic made the tapestry come to life, and she in turn had become a real human being.

Anna was overjoyed and invited her neighbors to live with her on her new land, for there were gardens and crops in abundance. Perrin and the young lady in red were married, and she took the name Eve.

A few months later, Leon and Blaine returned from the city, having spent all their money. They met Perrin and Eve upon the road. The two brothers gazed in amazement at the changed landscape before them.

"Mother's dream has come true," Perrin said in answer to their questioning looks.

"But why are you leaving?" asked Blaine.

Perrin looked at Eve and then replied, "The world is wide, and we have our own dreams to follow."

And so the two brothers begged forgiveness from their mother and lived with her once more. But Perrin and Eve explored the world, sang for beggars and kings alike, and wandered to their heart's content, as minstrels are wont to do.

First Edition

Author's Note

This story is mainly retold from the Chinese story "The Magic Brocade," with a number of elements adapted from the Norwegian tale "The Princess on the Glass Hill." As I felt my style is not especially suited to a Chinese setting, I moved the story to Europe during the fifteenth century, a period of elaborate tapestry making.

Library of Congress Cataloging-in-Publication Data

Sanderson, Ruth
  The crystal mountain / retold and illustrated by Ruth Sanderson. — 1st ed.
    p.   cm.
  Summary: The youngest of three sons outwits the fairy thieves who stole his mother's tapestry and marries one of the fairies who had helped him.
    ISBN 0-316-77092-2
    [1. Fairy tales.   2. Folklore.]   I. Title.
  PZ8.S253Gr   1999
  398.22 — dc21
  [E]   97-46991

10 9 8 7 6 5 4 3 2 1

NIL

Printed in Italy

The paintings for this book were done in oil on canvas.
The text was set in Truesdell, and the display type is Eva Antiqua and Basilica.